Stinky!

OR 'How the Beautiful Smelly Warthog Found a Friend'

For my beautiful smelly babies,
Suzannah and Lucy
I.W.

For John, my warmest supporter
and most honest critic, with love x
L.C.

Text first published in Great Britain in 1999 by Doubleday as
Whiff or How the Beautiful Big fat Smelly Baby Found a Friend

First published in Great Britain in 2009 by Gullane Children's Books
This paperback edition published in 2010 by
Gullane Children's Books
185 Fleet Street, London EC4A 2HS
www.gullanebooks.com

3   5   7   9   10   8   6   4   2

Text © Ian Whybrow 1999, 2009
Illustrations © Lynne Chapman 2009

The right of Ian Whybrow and Lynne Chapman to be identified as the author and illustrator of this
work has been asserted by them in accordance with the Copyright, Designs and Patents Act, 1988.
A CIP record for this title is available from the British Library.

ISBN: 978-1-86233-759-6

Printed and bound in China

Stinky!

OR 'How the Beautiful Smelly Warthog Found a Friend'

Ian Whybrow • Lynne Chapman

GULLANE
CHILDREN'S BOOKS

By a bend in the river lived a beautiful smelly baby warthog.
His mum and dad were very proud of him. They called him Stinky.
They wanted him to make friends and be happy.

The Crocodiles lived on one side. The
Monkeys lived on the other side. And right
across the river lived the Littlebirds.

One day Mrs Crocodile knocked on the door. She said, "My baby wants to play with your baby. But tell me, is your baby . . . rough?"

Mrs Warthog smiled and she said, "Ah no, my baby is NEVER rough."

So Stinky went next door to
play with Baby Crocodile.
He played very, very gently.

But then, because Stinky was a bit smelly . . .

...down came some tickly quickly flies!

They tickled their ears and
they tickled their eyes.

So the Crocodile bit his teddy bears,
he bashed the table
and he crashed the chairs!

His teeth went SNAP!
and his tail went w h e e e!
DOWN fell the pictures, one-two-three!

And Mrs Crocodile was very cross. She said to Stinky,
"Look what you've done! Go away!
You are much too rough to play!"

So Stinky the beautiful smelly baby
was sent home in disgrace.

Still, next day there was another knock
at the door. It was Mrs Monkey. She said,
"My babies would like your baby to come to tea.
But tell me, has your baby got nice table manners?"

Mrs Warthog smiled and said,
"Ah yes, my baby has got
LOVELY table manners."

So Stinky went next door to have tea with the Monkey babies.

He was on his best behaviour, but he was very smelly, and . . .

...down came the tickly quickly flies!

They tickled their ears and they tickled their eyes.
Cups and plates flew through the air,
and drinks went flying everywhere!

The three little monkeys
went jumping and squealing,
and jelly and custard
got stuck on the ceiling.

And Mrs Monkey was VERY VERY cross!
She said to Stinky, "Look at this mess! You can't stay!
Bad-mannered baby, go away!"

So Stinky the beautiful smelly baby was sent home in disgrace.

For a long time it seemed that Stinky would never find a friend.

Then one day, there
came a little teeny tap at
the door. It was Mrs Littlebird.
"My baby would like to play
with your baby," she said. "But
tell me, is your baby a good baby?"

Poor Mrs Warthog, she looked very anxious. She said,
"I think he is a VERY good baby, but Mrs Crocodile
says he is rough, and Mrs Monkey says he is
bad-mannered. They sent him home in disgrace!"

Mrs Littlebird did a little hop and a jump.
"I can see he is very beautiful," she said.
"But tell me, is he *always* smelly?"
"Always," said Mrs Warthog, proudly.

"Right!" said Mrs Littlebird. "Send him over!"

So Stinky went across the river to play with Baby Littlebird. They played happily for hours and hours. They played trains, planes, doctors and Jungle Monopoly.

But then…

...down came the tickly quickly flies!

They tickled their ears and they tickled their eyes. "Oh NO!" cried Stinky, "I must leave this place. For very soon I shall be in DISGRACE."

JUNGLE

Poor Stinky! He was terribly upset.
"I am rough," he sobbed. "I am bad-mannered!"

"NOT TO US," smiled Mrs Littlebird.
"You don't need to go away! My little baby would LOVE you to stay!
You are a beautiful smelly baby – and what a good thing
you are so smelly!" she smiled.
And all of a sudden, with a ...

SNIP!

SNAP!

SNUP!

The baby bird ate
all the flies up!

Baby Littlebird flapped her wings for joy.
"Yum, yum!" she sang.
"Can you come and play again tomorrow?"

And THAT is how the beautiful
smelly warthog found a friend.